Come along with us as
Trex learns
about embracing his
difference and what makes
every dinosaur
beautiful & unique!

Hello!
I am
Trex!

I'm learning how to read!
Will you help me
read this book?
You will?!
Yahoo!

Mama T. Rex roars, "Don't forget to make you bed!"

That's hard to do when your arms are smaller than your head!

4

You can YANK AND PULL!!

Maybe use your FEET?

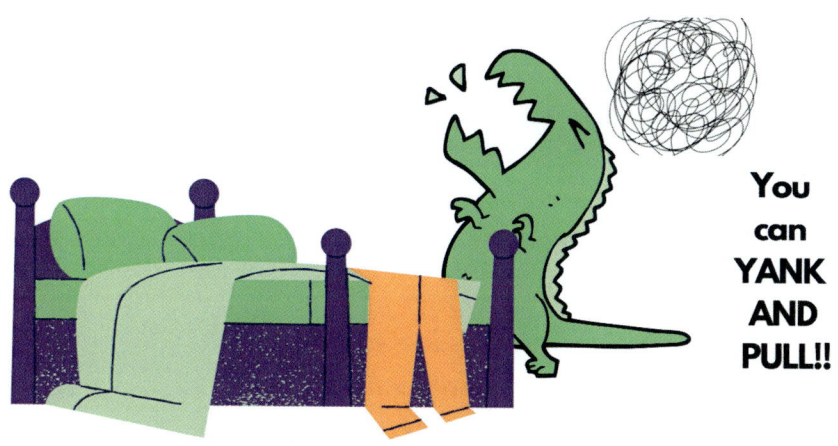

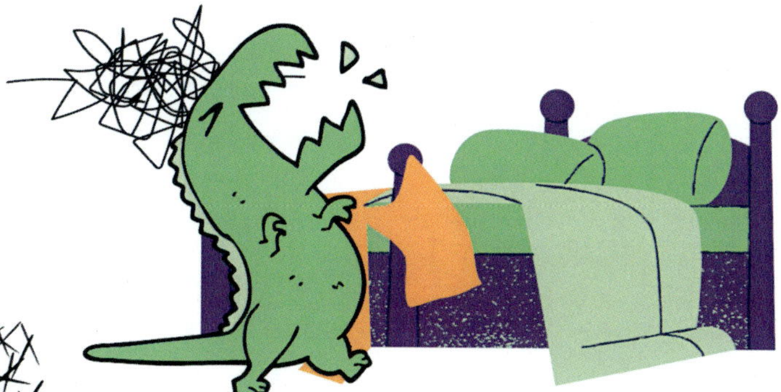

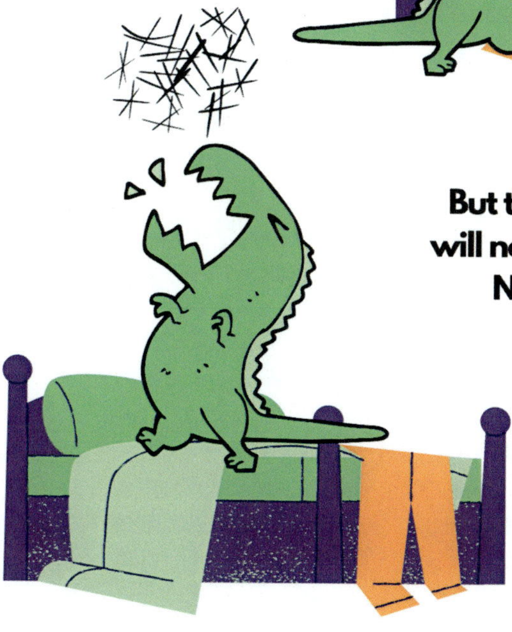

But that bed will never look NEAT!

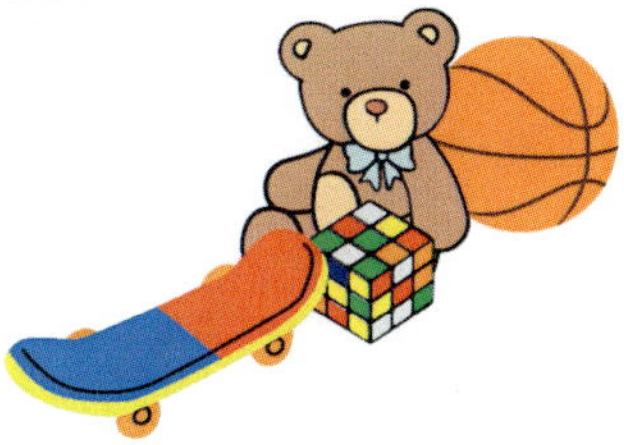

I wandered out to wait for the bus.
Tried to wave at my friend the diplodocus.
But he's got a neck that's way too tall,
and my T. rex arms are just
way too small!

I came home from school looking quite sad.
"Why the glum face?" asked my Tyrannosaurus rex dad.

I explained all my friends were awesome girls and cool guys!

How triceratops had three horns and pterodactyls could fly!
And brontosaurus could eat leaves high up in a tree!
But there was nothing...yes, absolutely nothing
special about me!

Mama sat down and snuggled me near.
And said "you are just as special my dear!
You're the biggest of Dinos, you should be quite proud!
You stand VERY tall and can ROAR very loud!

DO'S

**NOTHING
NOTHING
NOTHING**

DON'TS

**PUSH UPS
RIDE A BIKE
SWIMMING
DON'T DO ANYTHING**

With a sad little sigh said,
"I can't do fun things at all!
All because my arms are too small!
No push-ups, no bike rides or swimming
at the beach. All because my little arms won't reach!"

Mama T. Rex
shook her head and said, "awe, now you see,
you are very special to
Daddy and me!
A T. Rex's arms have always been small.
Maybe not made for swimming or ball.
But that's how we've been from the very start.
Just so I could hold you close to my heart!"

18

DRAW A PICTURE
WHAT MAKES YOU SPECIAL!

WRITE DOWN

WHAT DO YOU FIND UNIQUE ABOUT YOURSELF!

HAVE A BIG DINO HELP!

Dedicated To:
The three special Dinos in my life.
My children,
McKenna, Liam & Trex.
I am so blessed to be your Mama!

THE END

Made in United States
Orlando, FL
27 May 2023